TARO
and
the
Bamboo
Shoot

TARO and the Bamboo Shoot

A Japanese Tale
by Masako Matsuno
Illustrated by Yasuo Segawa
Adapted from the Japanese
by Alice Low

PANTHEON

Many, many years ago, a boy named Taro lived in a small village deep in the mountains of Japan. Thick groves of bamboo and dense forests of pine grew around it like a green wall, and cut the village off from the world beyond.

Once—so it was said—there had been a path to the far-off sea, but little by little the path had grown over, and the mountain people had become afraid to venture forth for fear of losing their way. At last, the path disappeared entirely; nobody ever left the village; nobody had ever seen that distant sea.

Life there was quiet and unchanging, until the day of Taro's ninth birthday.

That morning his mother said, "Taro, go and dig up a bamboo shoot. I'll make a special dish for you tonight."

So, licking his lips, Taro went to the bamboo grove behind his house to dig for a small tender shoot. Those which had already grown tall were too tough to eat.

He looked and looked, and at last he found a nice one.

"This is it!" he shouted excitedly and began digging around it. After a while he became very warm, so he took off his coat and hung it over another shoot that had just sprung up behind him.

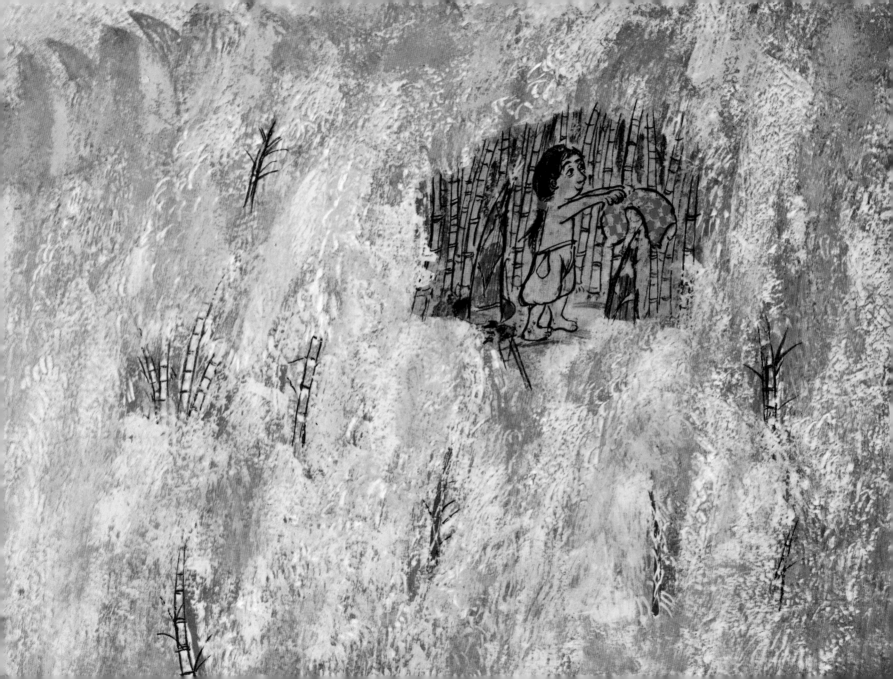

At that very moment the shoot started growing
miraculously fast—*whoosh* it went—taking Taro's coat
with it.

"My coat!" shouted Taro, and as he jumped up
to get it the shoot grew faster still. Up the shoot he
climbed, very quickly, but the faster he climbed
the faster it grew.

When at last he reached the top and
looked down, he became very frightened,
for he was ridiculously high up
above the ground.

After a while Taro's mother became uneasy and went to the bamboo grove to look for him. Imagine how she felt when she found only his straw sandals and hoe lying on the ground!

"Taro-o-o, Taro-o-o!" she called with all her might.

"Here…" came a voice from somewhere far above.

Then Taro's mother noticed that the bamboo shoot beside her was growing fast before her very eyes.

"Help! Help!" she screamed and called Taro's father.

Taro's father came running
and so did his next-door uncle
and aunt, and his next-next-door
uncle and aunt, and his friends and neighbors too. From
far and near, all the people of the village ran to help.

"Taro-o-o!" they called.

"Here…" came the answer, so faint they could hardly hear it.

"Taro-o-o!" they called again. But even as they called, the bamboo shoot became taller and taller and the trunk larger and larger.

"Let us cut it down," said Taro's father. "There is nothing else to do."

But this was of no use, for as they chopped, the trunk became larger still. And way up high, the tip swayed gently in the breeze—growing taller all the time—until suddenly, the shoot decided to take a rest.

"Look!" said Taro's father. "It has stopped growing. Now is the time to chop it down."

"Taro-o-o!" his father shouted.

"Ye-e-s...?"

"Hold on tight. We are going to cut the bamboo shoot now. Ready?"

"Rea—dy!" came the voice, far, far away.

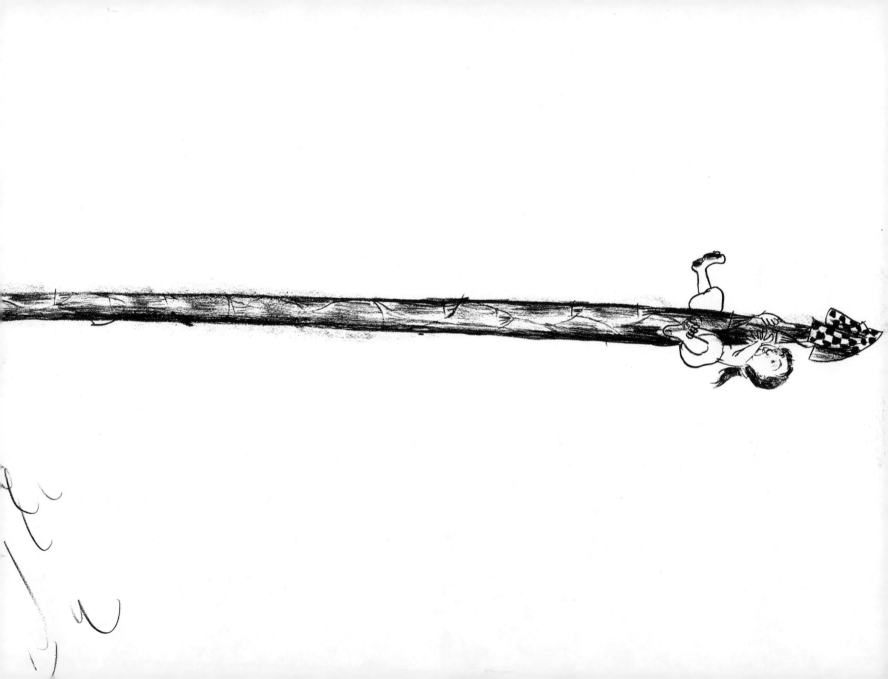

And after a great deal of chopping, the trunk was cut
through at last.

"*Wza-za-za-za…*" down it fell—down, down, down, with a
terrible swooshing noise—through many trees of tall bamboo,
through groves where oak and cedar grew, through forests dense
with stately pine, through mountains high and mountains low,
it cut its way the whole long day—on and on and on.

And all day long, Taro held on for his life.

All through the night he fell, his fingers stiff with cold, and
finally, when morning came, he felt a tremendous thump.

Meanwhile, at the other end, his father
and mother and uncles and aunts and friends and neighbors
listened all night long to the terrible swooshing noise.
The sun rose, morning came, and at last the bamboo shoot
fell to the ground with an awful final crash.

Everyone rushed forward,
fearing for Taro's life—
through many trees of tall bamboo,
through groves where oak and cedar grew,
through forests dense with stately pine,
through mountains high and mountains low,
they ran all day, the whole long way—
on and on and on.

And finally, toward evening, they came upon a great stretch of gleaming sand.

What a sight! White sand stretching and stretching, to right and to left. And in front of them, as far as they could see, a great, far-reaching pond.

And there on the sand lay Taro—quite still.

"Taro-o!" called his mother. "Wake up! Wake up!"

"He has fainted!" shouted his father. "Water! Water!" and he ran to the pond, scooped up a handful of water, and dashed it in Taro's face.

Taro sat up blinking.

Everyone hugged each other and cried for joy.

Taro cried too, and Taro's mother embraced him, crying all the while.

"Mother, could you please stop crying?" said Taro. "Your tears drip into my mouth and they are awfully salty!"

"Those are not my tears," said his mother. "Those are drops of water from the pond."

"Well, either way," said Taro, "they're awfully salty!"

"Salty pond water? How can it be?" said his next-door uncle, and he ran to the pond and took a big swallow.

"It *is* salty," he cried. "It must be the sea! Come here, everyone. This is the sea!"

"The sea? The sea that's full of fish?" asked his next-next-door uncle, tasting it too.

"And seaweed and shellfish!" said his next-door aunt and his next-next-door aunt together.

Taro and his father and mother ran to the sea and tasted the water too.

And it *was* salty! It really was!

"Just as my great-grandmother told me," said Taro's mother.

"Beyond the high mountains and the low mountains lies the sea."

"It has been more than a hundred years since any of our villagers has journeyed to the sea," said Taro's father.

"But from now on, we can come as often as we like," said Taro's next-door uncle.

"And we'll never get lost, as long as we follow this bamboo shoot," shouted everyone, very excitedly.

"Show me a shellfish! Show me some seaweed! Can you really eat fish?" asked Taro.

"They say you can," said Taro's mother, "and that they are very good, too!"

"Are they really better than bamboo shoots?" asked Taro.

"Let's catch some and find out," said Taro's father and uncles.

So they made some fishing poles and climbed up on a rock and fished. Taro fished too, while the others filled their arms with shellfish and seaweed.

When they had gathered as much as they could carry, they started home. In twilight and in dark of night, through mountains high and mountains low, through forests dense with stately pine, through groves where oak and cedar grew,

through many trees of tall bamboo—
they walked and walked, on and on and on.
And they did not lose their way, for
they followed the wonderful bamboo
shoot all the way home.

The next night, everyone gathered for a huge feast in honor of Taro's birthday.

Such a feast! Fish, seaweed, shellfish, and bamboo shoots—far more delicious than Mother's special dish!

"A wonderful feast!" everyone said.

"The best we have ever had," added Taro's next-door uncle, "even though I swallowed a fishbone."

After that day, the people of the mountains cut a
new path along the wonderful bamboo shoot and
made many trips to the sea.

Taro's mother and father and uncles and aunts and
neighbors busied themselves there catching fish and
shellfish, and returned home prosperous and happy.

Taro and his friends helped them. But
often, they paused and looked out across
the wide blue sea, dreaming about the
distant lands that lay—so it was said—far,
far beyond.